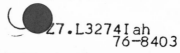

I Have
Four Names for
My Grandfather

I Have Four Names for My Grandfather

by
KATHRYN LASKY

Photographs by
CHRISTOPHER G. KNIGHT

LITTLE, BROWN AND COMPANY
BOSTON   TORONTO

c 8 Pet

I am indebted to Florence P. Rossman
for her special knowledge of young readers
that was so valuable to me in writing this book.

K. L.

TEXT COPYRIGHT © 1976 BY KATHRYN LASKY KNIGHT

PHOTOGRAPHS COPYRIGHT © 1976 BY CHRISTOPHER G. KNIGHT

FIRST EDITION

T 08/76

Library of Congress Cataloging in Publication Data

Lasky, Kathryn.
  I have four names for my grandfather.

  SUMMARY: A young boy describes his close
relationship with his grandfather.
  [1. Grandfathers — Fiction] I. Knight, .
Christopher G. II. Title.
PZ7.L3274Iah   [E]   76-8403
ISBN 0-316-51520-5

*Published simultaneously in Canada
by Little, Brown & Company (Canada) Limited*

PRINTED IN THE UNITED STATES OF AMERICA

To Martha

I have four names
for my grandfather.

I call him "Poppy"
and just plain "Pop."

I call him "Grandpa,"
and I call him "Gramps."

But with all four names

he's always the same grandfather for me.

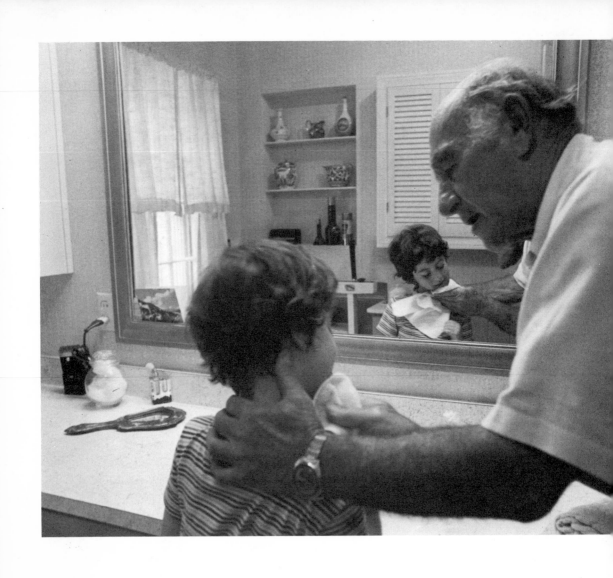

On his very top
Pop has no hair.
Not even one.

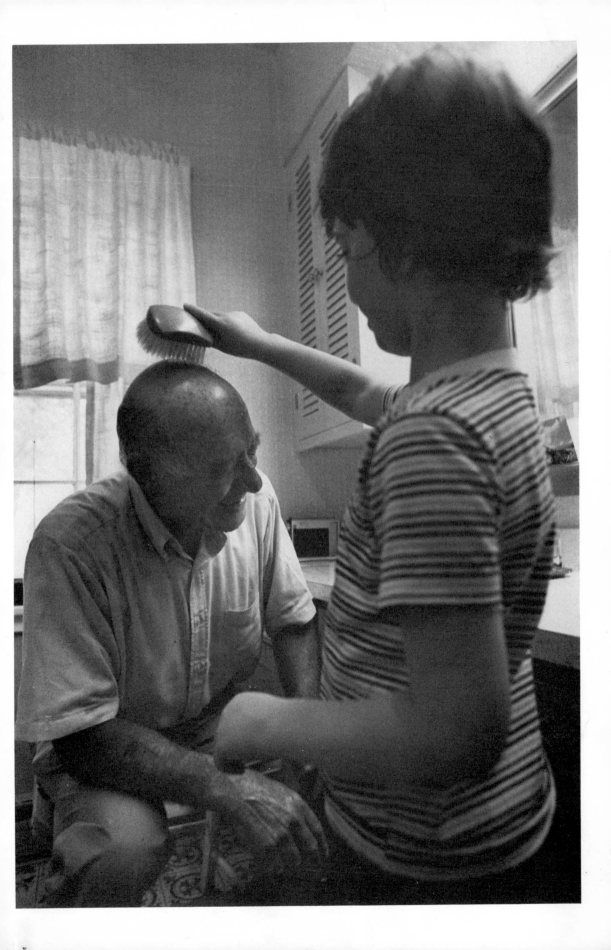

So he has lots of hats.
One for sun,
one for fun,
one for snow,
and one for show.

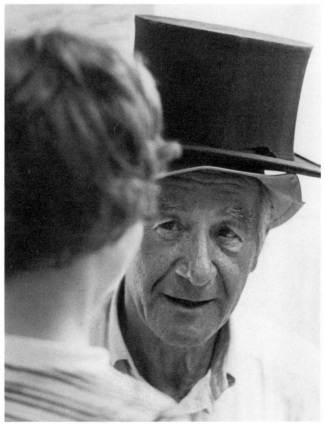

And Gramps lets me try some, too!

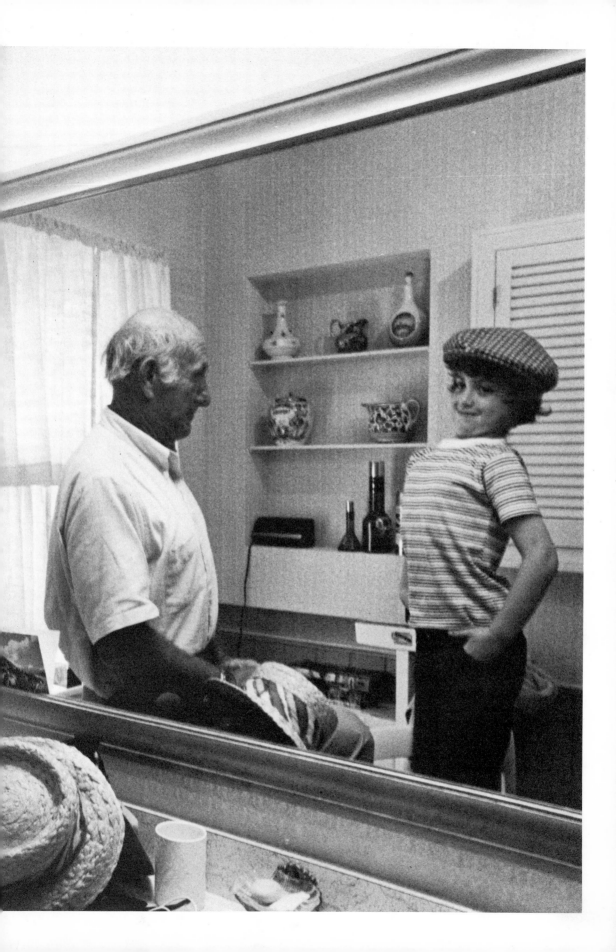

I'm as tall as Grandpa's pocket
and Gramp's nose is as long as my finger.

And look, my foot is
as big as Poppy's hand.

And this is neat—
Pop calls me "Big Foot,"
just for fun.

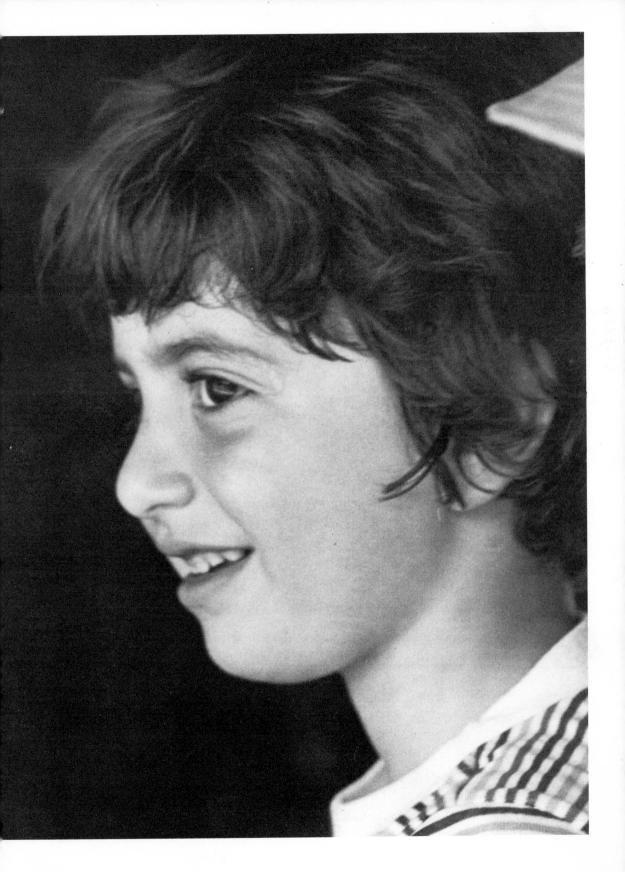

But my real name is Tom.

Grandpa and I, we play a lot.
He says to me: "Big Foot, let's run."
And off we go.

Sometimes we go and see an old train,

number five-eight-seven,
and pretend to make a run to Denver
or maybe Boston.

And sometimes we go fishing.
We catch lots of yucky things —
sticks and old balls
and hats and boots.

But once a fish —
a very small fish.

I put the fish in a jar,
and I wonder how long
it will live in there.
So I ask Pop:
"Will it die soon in there?"
"Not sure," he says.
"When will you die, Gramps?" I ask.
"How do I know?" he says.
"When will Bertie Turtle die?" I ask.
"Who knows?" Pop says.

Gramps hammers nails very well.
He helps me, but it is hard.
"Keep your eye on the nail, Tom," he says.
I try.

I really try.

And in May we plant flowers,
Gramps and me. He says my hands
are just right to dig the hole
and hold the plant
and pat the dirt around it.

Sometimes I say, "Pop, make a funny face."
First he makes a funny face.

And then I make one, too.

Then we play tickle pickle.

When I feel bad or mad
I can call up Pop.
His number is two-one-five-six-four-five-five.

I say, "Hi, Gramps, I am so angry!"
And he never asks if I was bad.

But best of all when I am sad,
Grandpa hugs me very close and says:
"I love you, Tom."